Graham Carter

OTTO BLOTTER

BIRD SPOTTER

Ⓐ
Andersen Press

Turtledove was a town much like any other,
except for one small difference...

it was FULL of birds and bird-spotters.

And the most famous
spotters were a family
named Blotter.

The Blotters spent every moment of every day spotting birds.

They'd even turned their home into the perfect hide
so they NEVER had to leave it.

But young Otto Blotter was NOT a spotter!

He didn't like staying indoors all day.

What he liked was to EXPLORE!

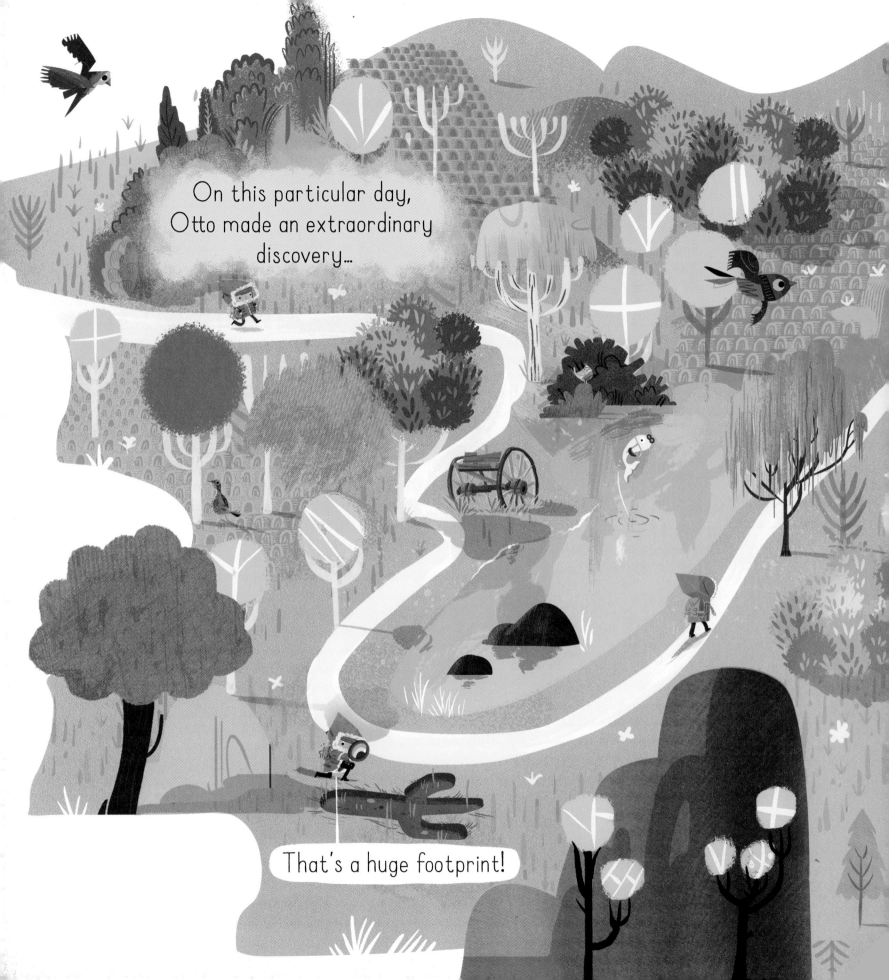

On this particular day, Otto made an extraordinary discovery...

That's a huge footprint!

Hidden in the bushes,
all alone, sat the most
unusual little BIRD.

Otto wasn't allowed pets, but he couldn't just leave the little fellow.
He scooped up Bird and sneaked him back to his room.
Luckily his family were too busy to notice.

The next day Otto took his feathery friend to all his favourite exploring spots.

And sneakily fed and bathed him after the rest of the family had gone to bed.

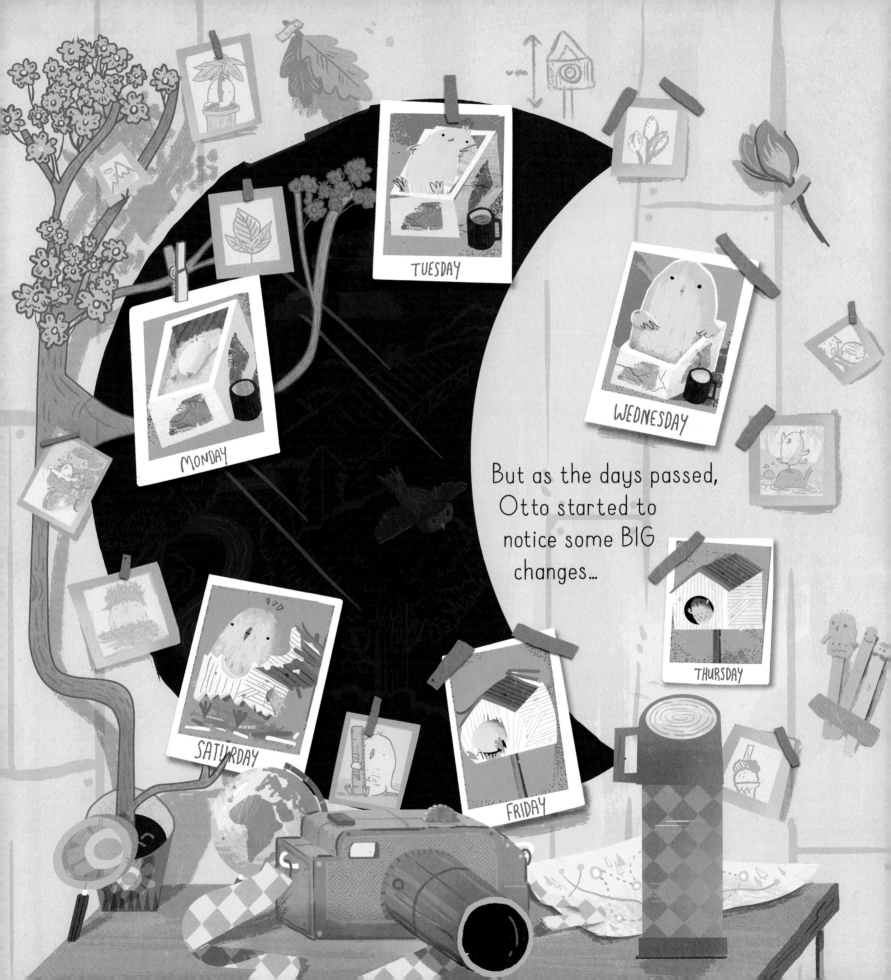

TUESDAY

MONDAY

WEDNESDAY

But as the days passed, Otto started to notice some BIG changes...

THURSDAY

SATURDAY

FRIDAY

His little friend was not so little any more.

And Otto's secret was becoming TOO BIG to hide.

Otto knew Bird was going to be
discovered any minute.
There was nothing more he could do
to hide his huge friend!

Luckily, Bird didn't like to see Otto upset. He knew this was the moment to show his friend something truly remarkable...

Good day Otto!

CAMOUFLAGE!

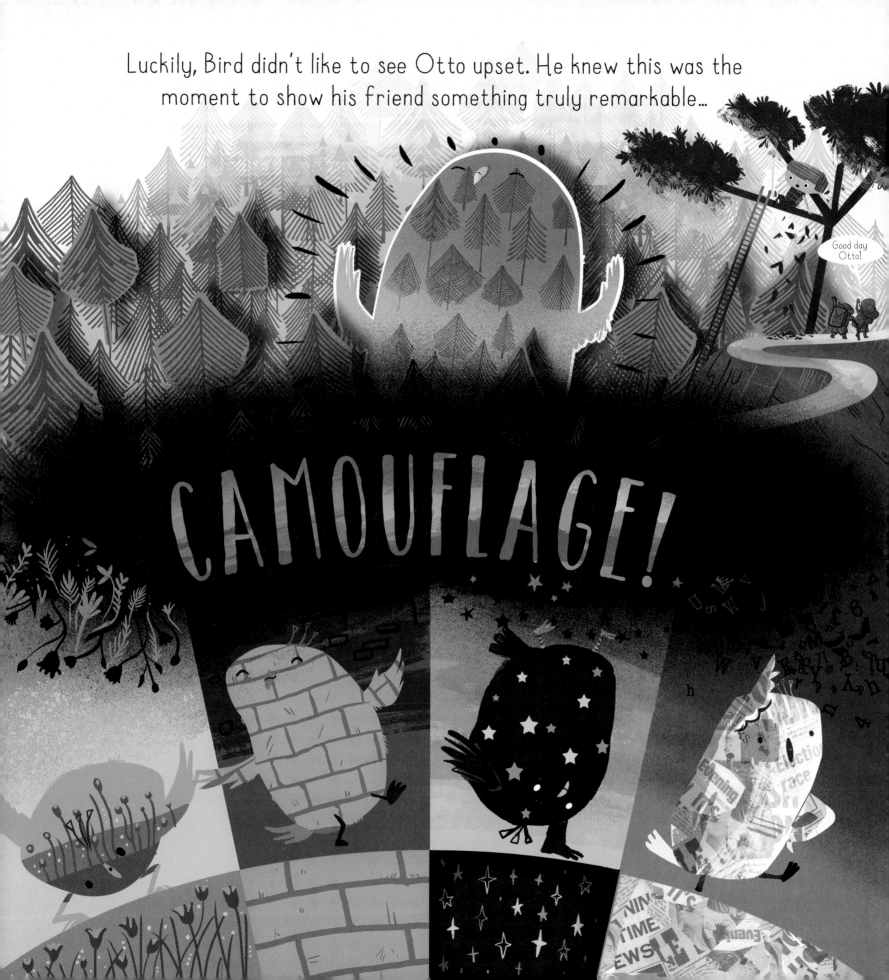

Otto was over the moon!

Now Bird could disguise himself as anything, it meant they could go anywhere.

They could once again visit their favourite spots and go on fabulous adventures.

And no one would ever know.

Otto and Bird could not have been happier, until the day they visited the zoo.

As they passed family after family of meerkats, penguins,

monkeys and stingrays, Bird seemed to grow sadder and sadder.

Otto's thoughts flashed back to the day he first found Bird:
the huge footprints, the giant feathers, the massive pile of poo…

Suddenly he realised:
Bird hadn't been alone.
Bird had a family!

But Otto was going to need help to find them.

Luckily, Otto's family were expert bird-spotters.

SURPRISE! Look who I found.

After recovering from meeting the most majestic bird ever discovered,
the whole Blotter family set to work helping Otto come up with a plan.

By nightfall they had made the tallest bird-spotting tower ever built.
The Blotters were sure they would spot Bird's family in no time now.

Then something magical happened. "FAMILY!" cried Bird,

glowing so brightly, he lit up the whole night.

In the distance, something began to rustle… something began to stir…

and something began to glow. One by one, three even bigger birds

came out of the darkness. They'd found them!

Otto was really happy
that his friend had
found his family.

But that didn't make it any easier when the time came to say goodbye.

The Blotters hoped they
would spot him again one day though.

After all – they were experts.

From that day on, Otto became a top spotter himself.

And the rest of the Blotters found that
exploring with Otto led to all kinds of amazing
discoveries (and the odd adventure).

For the rest of the Carter family – Alice, Noah and Finlay x

This paperback edition first published in 2020 by Andersen Press Ltd.
First published in 2019 by Andersen Press Ltd.,
20 Vauxhall Bridge Road, London, SW1V 2SA

1 3 5 7 9 10 8 6 4 2

British Cataloguing in Publication Data Available.

ISBN 978 1 78344 896 8